MORTON THE MAGICIAN

›AND HIS MAGNIFICENT MAGIC SHOW‹

Magic is believing in yourself; if you can do that, you can make anything happen.

Johann Wolfgang von Goethe

This is
MORTON
and he has a secret.

For as long as he
could remember, Morton
wanted to be a magician.

Morton was afraid that his
friends would make fun of him
if they knew he liked magic.

For years, he practiced alone, never
showing anyone his magic tricks.

Morton read every magic
book he could find. Short books,
long books, thin books, fat books.

He read the books with lightning speed,
leaving a trail of magic everywhere he went.

Desperate to find a magic book
→ he hadn't read before, ←
Morton made the familiar trip to the town

LIBRARY.

Morton had read every magic book on the shelves.
He was about to leave when he saw something out of the corner of his eye.
In the shadows of the empty shelf was a book that Morton had never seen before.

MAGIC

WONDER

ART OF MAGIC

Covered in **DUST**.

A MAGICIAN'S BEST FRIEND

DECEPTION

MAGIC 101

MARVELS OF MYSTERY

Covered in **COBWEBS**.

MARMOTS

This book had been hiding for **YEARS**! One more magic book for Morton to read.

HOUDINI THE UNTOLD STORY

Magical Secrets

MAGIC

Filled with excitement,
Morton opened the book.

To his delight, a
FURRY RABBIT
leaped out of the pages.

"I'm not just any talking rabbit! My name is Harry and I'm a real magician's assistant," said Harry. "I've been jumping out of magicians' hats for over 100 years. 5,789 appearances and counting!"

"That's incredible!" Morton exclaimed. "I want to be a magician. Can you be my magic rabbit too?"

Morton and Harry left the library and went home. Hoping to impress Harry, Morton showed off his best magic tricks.

➜ "When is your next performance?" Harry asked. ⬿

"Well, I don't actually show anyone my magic," replied Morton.

LOOK HARRY, I'M FLOATING!

Morton realized that Harry was right.
It was time to share his magic with the world.
It was time to put on a

MAGIC SHOW.

Magic
Show!!

Starring Morton
and Harry
THIS SATURDAY
tickets 25¢
Where: Morton's
Backyard

Everyone around town heard about
Morton's upcoming magic show.
But there were two problems...

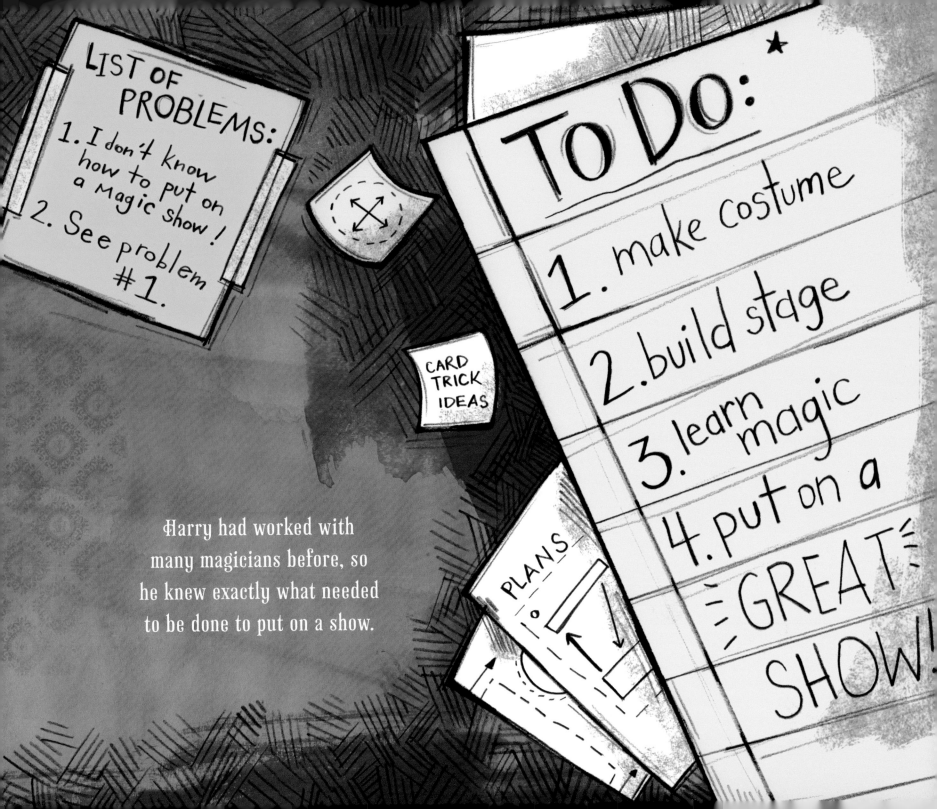

LIST OF PROBLEMS:

1. I don't know how to put on a Magic show!

2. See problem #1.

CARD TRICK IDEAS

PLANS

TO DO: ★

1. make costume

2. build stage

3. learn magic

4. put on a GREAT SHOW!

Harry had worked with many magicians before, so he knew exactly what needed to be done to put on a show.

If Morton was ever going to convince an audience that he was a real magician, he knew that he had to look like a real magician.

TO DO:
1. costume
2. build stage
learn
put on
EAT SHOW

With a needle, some thread, and a piece of shiny red satin fabric, the costume started to take shape.

From Broadway to the Las Vegas Strip, Harry had assisted magicians on the world's finest stages.

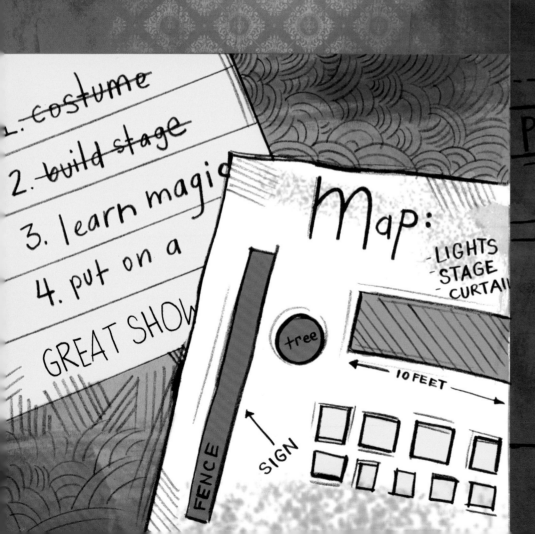

1. costume
2. build stage
3. learn magic
4. put on a
GREAT SHOW

Map:
- LIGHTS
- STAGE
- CURTAIN
tree
10 FEET
FENCE
SIGN

PLAN

?

But none were as rustic and unique as the one in Morton's backyard.

Plywood, duct tape,
and bed sheets never
looked so good.

Morton and Harry were inseparable.
They spent every moment together
daydreaming about the fantastic feats
they would perform in the magic show.

★ TODO:
1. make costume
2. build stage
3. learn magic
4. put on a
GREAT SHOW!

With his notebook in hand, Morton filled page after page with ideas for his show.

Coming up with amazing tricks was easy – learning the secrets was the hard part.

RISING CARD

THE TRICK

Make a card mysteriously rise out of the deck.

THINGS NEEDED

Deck of playing cards

SECRET

Hold the deck of cards in your left hand with the cards facing the audience. Extend your right hand's pointer finger and rest it on top of the deck. Secretly extend your right hand's pinkie finger and push it on the back of the deck. When the right hand lifts up, the pinkie finger will secretly push up the back card of the deck. It will appear as if the card is magically rising beneath the pointer finger.

REMEMBER

The deck of cards hides the secret pinkie finger from the audience, so make sure the audience isn't watching from the sides.

INSTANT FREEZE

THE TRICK

Turn water into ice in 3 seconds flat!

THINGS NEEDED

Small glass of water

Empty coffee cup

Sponge

Ice cube

SECRET

Before the performance, put the secret sponge in the bottom of the cup and then put an ice cube on top of it. During the performance, pour the water into the cup. The sponge will absorb the water. Say the magic words and tip the cup upside down so the ice cube will fall out. The water will stay inside the cup because of the sponge.

REMEMBER

Test how much water the sponge will hold before performing the trick.

Don't let anyone see inside the cup. If they see the sponge, the trick will be ruined.

Put the cup away while the audience is applauding, or else they may want to look at the cup.

The costume was on... the stage was set... the tricks were ready... and the audience was taking their seats. Excitement and anticipation filled the air.

———◆———

Morton never felt this nervous before. Butterflies filled his stomach and stage fright filled his thoughts. Morton waited backstage and made sure all of his props were firmly placed up his sleeve.

———◆———

Harry said, "I believe in you, kid. Don't worry – Harry Houdini felt nervous before his first show too!"

WILL MY FRIENDS MAKE FUN OF ME?

WILL THE AUDIENCE LIKE THE SHOW?

WILL I REGRET SHOWING OTHERS MY MAGIC?

WILL THE MAGIC WORK?

...children of all ages, welcome
to the Magnificent Magic Show.
Prepare to be amazed and dazzled by...

MORTON THE MAGICIAN!

Morton's nervousness disappeared the moment he stepped onto the stage.

Magic flowed effortlessly from his fingertips and the audience cheered with shouts of amazement.

WHOO!
WHOO!

TA-DA!

The audience leaped
to their feet. A standing
ovation for Morton!

Everyone loved Morton's
magic and the show was
a stunning success.

I THINK MY WORK HERE IS DONE...

"Harry, I couldn't have done this show without you. You made me into the magician I've always wanted to be," Morton said.

"Don't be silly," said Harry. "You always were an amazing magician. You just didn't believe that you were. All you needed was the courage and confidence to share your magic with others. Believe in yourself, kid – that is the biggest secret of all!"

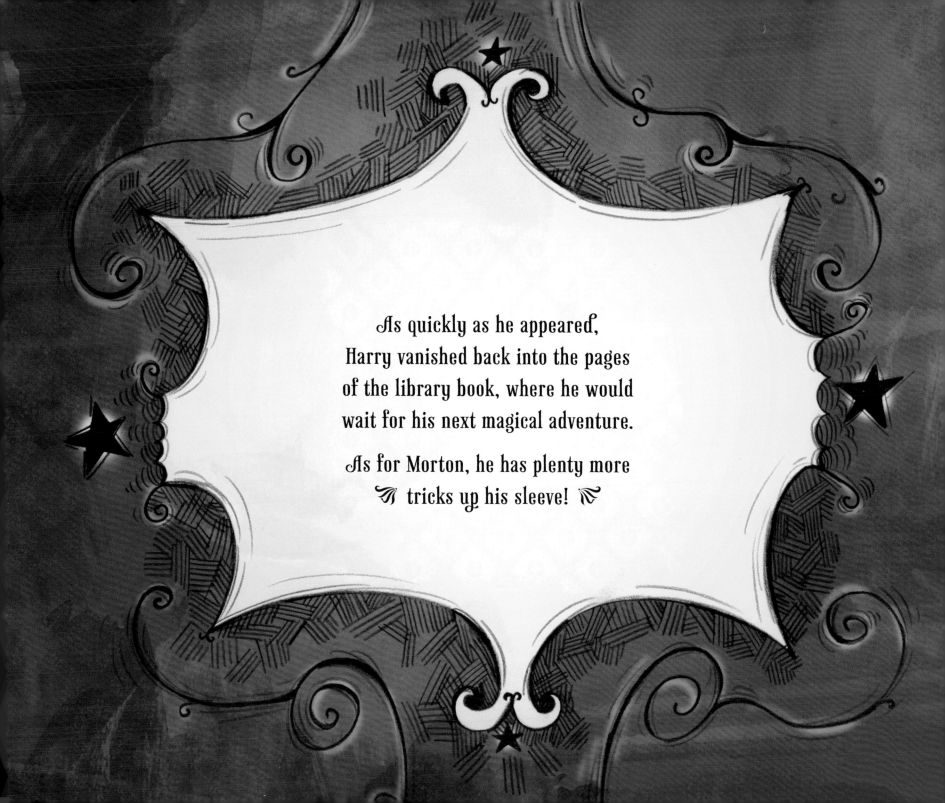

As quickly as he appeared,
Harry vanished back into the pages
of the library book, where he would
wait for his next magical adventure.

As for Morton, he has plenty more
tricks up his sleeve!